Book 1
Clancy the Quokka
of
Rottnest Island

Jonathan Macpherson
Copyright © 2019 by Jonathan Macpherson.
All Rights Reserved.

Chapter 1

The first rays of the morning sun shone through the hole in the roof of the cave, creating a soft light over the white sandy floor. Clancy's eyes flickered open and he rubbed them with his paw, waking up. He looked around the cave and saw all the other quokkas still fast asleep in their little corners and nooks, some of them huddled together. Clancy's mother lay on her side nearby, a little quokka nose poking out from her pouch which belonged to his baby sister, Emma, who was just a few days old. Behind his mother, Clancy's father snored in a deep sleep.

Clancy loved being the first to wake up; there was something special about it.

He leaned back onto his hind legs and stretched his front paws towards the roof high above, then hopped across the sandy floor to a small spring of water. He had a drink then took a pawful of water and washed his furry face. Wide awake now, he hopped along the edge of the stream, following it out through the entrance to a sand dune. Clancy sat back on his haunches, overlooking a stunning beach. He was only a youngster, and there was much of Rottnest Island he had not yet explored. But so far, the beach right outside his clan's cave was his very favourite place. The Basin, as the beach was known, had soft white sand and pristine turquoise water. It was flanked on the left and right by tall, rocky

1

outcrops, which protected it from rough seas, and kept the water calm and flat most of the time.

Clancy snapped a leaf off a tree and munched on it as he hopped down the dune to the beach. He walked along the water's edge. Like most quokkas, he had never been swimming before.

"Quokkas are land creatures," his father had told him, "and unless you want to end up in a seal's belly, you'd better stay on land. Young quokkas make a perfect seal meal, I've seen it before. A little quokka frolicking in the water, then *swish!* Taken, fast as lightning. Never seen again."

This story had frightened Clancy enough to keep him out of the water, but he couldn't stay away from the beach, and loved to stroll along the water's edge. The sun was already quite warm and the water was still and so clear he could see the white sand at the bottom. It looked very inviting. He had never seen a seal, and his friend Cobba had told him seals lived on the other side of the island.

I'll just go in a little way, just get my paws wet, he thought. He looked around, checking that there weren't any other quokkas about, then Clancy waded in. The cool, refreshing water was more wonderful than he had imagined, and he was sure it would be even more wonderful if he went for a swim. *What harm could come from a little dip? The water is so clear, I'll spot a seal coming from miles away!*

Convinced it was safe, he waded out a bit deeper so the lovely water came up to his chest. *Paradise!* he thought, and ducked his head under the water. It was magical. So cool, so pleasant, like nothing he'd ever experienced. He rolled onto his back, and discovered that he could float. Paddling with his hind legs, he put his front paws behind his head and propelled himself along in the shallows. *This is the life,* he thought.

Then something under the water brushed against his back, sending fear shuddering through him. He stood up in the chest-deep water and got a fright. Lying right in front of him, just below the surface of the water, was a black stingray. Though he was relieved it wasn't a seal, he was still a bit nervous. He'd seen plenty of stingrays from the beach, but had never been up this close to one before. He had heard how stingrays could kill with their barbed tails if they felt threatened, so he decided to keep perfectly still. The ray flapped its wing-like fins, making gentle ripples in the water. It seemed to be saying hello, and Clancy thought it was only polite to reply.

"Hi there," he said, "I'm Clancy."

The stingray lifted its head above the water, its large eyes looking right at Clancy. They were friendly eyes, and they beamed in a way that Clancy was sure meant the stingray was smiling. It flapped its wings some more, then stopped as if waiting for Clancy to respond.

"How are you?" Clancy said, and the ray responded with a short burst of ripples, then stopped. Clancy put his front paws in the water and splashed up and down in a gentle rhythm, producing a similar set of ripples. Then he stopped, and it was the stingray's turn. They continued like this for a while, and Clancy was surprised to find they could understand each other, in a basic sort of way.

"Do you live in the Basin?" Clancy asked, tapping his paws in the water in a way that he hoped corresponded with his words.

The ray shook its head.

"Do you live nearby?" he asked, still tapping.

The ray nodded its head for *yes*. Then it curved its tail around and Clancy could see it had some fishing line wrapped around it.

"Want me to try and get that off?" he said, tapping his hands in the water.

The ray nodded, and Clancy gently examined the tail, unravelling the line until he came to the end, which was attached to a fish hook, pinned through the ray's skin.

"This is going to hurt. Are you sure you want me to pull it out?" he said, tapping away.

The ray nodded.

Clancy realised if he pulled the hook back out the way it came in, it would do even more damage to the ray's tail. He thought it might be less painful to pull it out the other way, so the sharp barb didn't make contact with the ray's skin. Careful not to prick himself, he pulled it through, and the ray jerked a little, reacting to the pain. But soon the worst was over, and Clancy pulled the line through, paw over paw, until he had completely removed it from the tail. The ray nuzzled its head into Clancy's tummy, like he was hugging him. Clancy patted him on the back.

"You're welcome," Clancy said.

Then the ray sprang around, facing the open water, where a seal was speeding towards them along the surface. Clancy's mouth fell open. *A seal! Here, in the Basin!* He turned and bounded out of the water. From the safety of the beach, Clancy could see the stingray zooming away in the clear, shallow water.

"Oh, no!" Clancy said, as the seal gave chase. He'd never seen creatures move so fast. The seal sped along like a torpedo, gaining on the stingray, following it out into the darker, deeper water.

Then the seal circled back, bobbing in and out of the water, and Clancy realised the stingray must have got away.

"Phew," Clancy sighed, shaking his furry coat and getting most of the water off. He hopped up the dune, then looked back down to the water. The ray and the seal were nowhere to be seen, but he was sure the ray was safe.

What a morning, he thought. His first ever swim, his first meeting with a stingray, and his first terrifying encounter with a seal! *What next?*

Clancy continued up the dune when he saw a flash in the corner of his eye. He turned just in time to see something flying through the air in his direction.

Chapter 2

There was no time to duck out of the way, but he was able to raise his front paws and protect himself, just as the quokka crashed into him. The two of them rolled down the soft sand. When they stopped, the other quokka was sitting on top of Clancy and laughing hysterically. It was his best mate, Cobba, and he had caught Clancy by surprise, once again.

"Good morning!" Cobba said, smiling.

Clancy tried to get out from under Cobba, wriggling and squirming, but it was no use, he was pinned down.

"Give up?" Cobba asked, brushing his whiskers under Clancy's chin and tickling him.

There was no way Clancy was going to give up to Cobba, or anyone else for that matter. Desperate to escape, he raised his hind legs and managed to wriggle his toes under Cobba's armpits. He tucked his feet, or rather his paws, right under, then thrust his powerful back legs upwards, sending Cobba flying.

"Wooooaaah!" Cobba yelled, sailing through the air then landing on a bush. "That was fun!"

"How long have you been awake?" Clancy asked.

"I haven't been to sleep yet," Cobba said, beaming with pride.

Clancy was amazed. Everyone else in the clan tended to go to bed at around midnight and sleep all the way until lunchtime the following day, sometimes even later.

"What have you been up to?" Clancy asked.

"Just exploring, hanging out with the tourists, taking selfies."

"Selfies?"

"Yeah. Come on, I'll show you."

Intrigued, Clancy followed Cobba up to the top of the dune where the grass was thick and, after checking that no people were around, they ducked into a secret quokka tunnel that had been burrowed into the grass. They hopped down the tunnel, the sun shining through the gaps in the grass that arched overhead. Along the way, Clancy told Cobba about his encounters with the stingray and the seal.

"No way! A seal?"

"Yeah! And you said they didn't come to this side of the island."

"There's a first time for everything," Cobba said. "Wow, I'd love to have some fun like that. Maybe we could go around the island exploring, and have some adventures."

"Around the island?"

"Yeah! Did you know there are lots of different quokka clans all over the island?"

"Yes, of course."

"But did you know they're very different from us?"

"Really?"

"Oh, yeah! My dad told me all about them. And not all of the clans are friendly. Take the Narrow Neck Clan, boy they're some tough nuts. You don't want to rub them up the wrong way, that's for sure. They think our little Basin Clan is as soft as sea sponge."

"Really? Why is that?"

"Well, we're so protected from the weather, and life's so peaceful here. They're probably right, I guess. The Thomson Bay Clan is a different mob altogether. Being in the centre of town, they're quick-witted quokkas, real hustlers, talk you out of your lunch before you can say "g'day"."

"Wow, I had no idea."

"Oh, that's just the half of it. There's the Eagle Bay Clan, who are super sporty; the West End Clan, very dramatic; the Stark Bay Clan, they love the winter; I could go on and on," he said, as they emerged from the grassy tunnel to a sheltered barbecue area on a beach, where about half a dozen people were sitting on benches in the shade.

Clancy was still a little nervous about people and had not yet met one. Even though people had a reputation for being the friendliest animals on the island, they were also very large and powerful, even the young ones. In fact, the young ones seemed to be more dangerous than the bigger ones, always running about in all directions with no regard for who or what they might bump into. Clancy had even seen a child picking up a poor, unlucky quokka. He certainly did not want to be picked up!

He stood back and watched in admiration as Cobba strode right up to the group of people. Before long they were gathering around and fawning over him, making all sorts of affectionate noises.

Cobba spoke to Clancy in a series of clicks with his tongue, the sounds of the native quokka language. Even though quokkas understand human language and often speak it among themselves, they never do so in front of humans. So to the people gathered near Clancy and Cobba, their conversation sounded like ticks, tooks, tucks and clicks.

"Come on over; they're super friendly!" Cobba said.

"Yes, I can see that. Maybe a little too friendly."

"They won't hurt you. Come on."

Clancy tottered over beside Cobba, and soon he was the subject of plenty of fawning. A man crouched down, his head right next to Clancy's, and held a contraption out in front of him. Clancy found the smell of the man a bit strong and unpleasant.

"It's a phone," Cobba said, "he wants to take a selfie. Look!" Cobba said, pointing to the screen, where Clancy could see his face next to the man's face. There was a *click* and the man inspected the image on his phone and seemed quite pleased with it.

"Nice one," Cobba said, as some of the other people began leaning down over both of the quokkas. They suddenly seemed to be all around them in a way that was uncomfortable. Feeling uneasy, Clancy darted between their legs, and hopped away from the group. He hopped over to the tunnel, ready to bolt if the humans persisted. But they must have sensed his discomfort and left him alone. Cobba was providing more than enough entertainment; Clancy had never seen his friend smile so much. Cobba was truly in his element.

Clancy sat beneath the shade of a tree, happy to watch as Cobba soaked up all the attention.

"Excuse me," came a tiny voice behind him. Clancy turned to see a young quokka, only a toddler, and about half Clancy's size, quivering next to him.

"Hey, what's wrong?"

"Do you know where my mum is?"

"What's her name?"

"Quinlynn."

"No, sorry, I don't know Quinlynn," Clancy said. "See those quokkas over by that bush? Why don't you hop along and ask them? They might be able to help. Okay? Bye now," Clancy said, and the little quokka sniffed and hopped away.

Another man approached Clancy and crouched beside him, his phone in hand. Clancy wasn't in the mood and looked away. Then he noticed a juicy slice of carrot hanging in mid air right in front of his face. He leaned forward to sniff the delicious looking carrot, which was dangling from the man's hand. It swung gently around, Clancy following it with his nose so he was soon facing the phone, his face beside the man's face. He knew he had been tricked into another selfie, but the carrot looked so juicy, he didn't mind. The man dangled it just out of reach, and kept snapping away until finally he lowered it for Clancy, who opened his mouth. As he chomped down, he heard a *swoosh*. His mouth closed but he hadn't bitten anything. The carrot had disappeared. Feeling cheated, he looked around and saw an old quokka standing beside him, the carrot on the ground nearby. Clancy reached for the carrot but before he could grab it, the old quokka whipped his tail around with lightning speed and flicked the carrot away.

"Don't take their food," the old quokka said, his voice deep and raspy.

The old quokka had a fearsome look about him. His fur was sun bleached and he had some old scars across his chest and face that looked like they had come from fighting.

"I–"

"Don't," the old quokka said, with a hint of anger. "And when a youngster needs help, you must do your best to help them. Don't hope that someone else will. We quokkas need to take care of each other." With that he turned and slowly hopped away.

Cobba hopped up beside Clancy. "What happened? You look like you've seen a snake."

"He just knocked that juicy carrot right out of my hand," Clancy said, gesturing to the old quokka, who disappeared into the quokka tunnel. "I didn't even see him coming."

"Oh, that's Van Cleef. He's one mean, tough old quokka. But he knows what he's talking about. If you want to stay healthy, stick to native vegetation. Didn't your parents ever teach you–"

"Yeah, yeah, I know. It was a moment of weakness."

"I knew you were weak, haha!"

"Don't start."

Cobba whacked Clancy's cheek with his tail. "Start what?"

"That's it!"

Cobba bolted and Clancy chased after him. They bounded up the nearby steps onto the bitumen road, into the path of four bicycles. Clancy skidded to a stop just a whisker away from a spinning pedal, and both he and Cobba dodged and weaved, the cyclists swerving and wobbling. They crossed the road, Clancy still in hot pursuit.

Cobba spotted a bicycle leaning against a tree, a picnic basket attached to the back. He leapt up onto the seat, then leapt onto the tree trunk. Clancy followed, leaping onto the picnic basket. He wanted to spring up to the tree after Cobba, but the lid of the basket collapsed under him and he fell inside. He rolled into the dark basket as the lid clapped shut above. He pushed up at the lid, but it wouldn't open. Pressing both front paws and his head against it, he used all his strength, but the cane basket lid would not budge. He was trapped.

Chapter 3

Clancy pushed up against the lid of the basket as hard as he possibly could, but it was shut tight. A heavy thud on the lid knocked him to the bottom of the basket.

"You okay?" called Cobba, who was now on top of the basket, having just jumped on and knocked Clancy down.

"Yes, I'm okay. But I can't get this open."

"Hang on, I'll get you out," Cobba said.

Clancy listened as Cobba struggled above him, puffing and panting, but unable to get the basket open.

"Oh no!" Cobba said, then leapt off the lid.

Clancy wondered what was wrong, but it was soon obvious as the basket heaved sideways and began to move. He pushed up against the lid once more, and though he couldn't open it, he noticed a gap. He peered through and could see Cobba standing on the road behind him, getting smaller as Clancy moved further away. He realised the owner of the bicycle was on the move. His eyes widened in panic and he lay on his back and put his hind legs on the basket lid, nose wrinkling as he pushed with all his might. But it was no good.

There was nothing he could do to escape, so he pushed his head up against the lid and looked out through the gap again. At least he could see where they were going, or rather, where they had gone, as he was facing backwards. Hopefully he would be able to find his way back home later. In the meantime, he would enjoy the thrill of riding on the back of a bicycle. He'd never moved so fast!

They rode for some time, along a beach Clancy had never seen before; through a collection of bungalows; beneath the tallest trees he'd ever seen; up and down hills and around winding bends. He realised that the further they rode, the trickier it would be to find his way home, though he knew somehow he would manage. What worried him was how his mother would react when he didn't show up for lunch, or dinner. He was sure she would be worried sick.

He poked his nose out under the lid, sniffing the air, smelling the familiar scents of wild flowers and plants along with some unfamiliar but delicious smells that he was sure came from food prepared by humans.

Children playing by the side of the road began to notice him, pointing and waving and calling out to him. Clancy was tempted to wave back, but knew very well that he mustn't break the quokka code and communicate with people. *Just as well there's no rule against smiling at them*, he thought, as he beamed from ear to ear.

Two small birds flew behind Clancy, just above his head. They tweeted and whistled at him, as if asking what he was doing in the basket. One bird was a golden whistler, the other a red-capped robin. Clancy had seen such birds darting about the island, but they were always going so fast he'd never had a chance to get a good look at them. He was so impressed by their striking and beautiful colours, he almost forgot to respond to them. He pointed to the lid above his head. *Tuk tic tuk-tuk*! He said, which meant he couldn't get out.

The birds dropped down a bit so they were so close, he thought he could probably reach out and touch them. He watched in awe as they managed to keep up with the bike while darting side to side and examining the rear of the basket. It looked so effortless, as if they were flying without trying, or just floating in the air.

They went to work on the latch at the back of the basket and, in a flash, the basket lid popped open above Clancy. He gave them the thumbs up and they whistled and winked at him, then shot away above the trees. Clancy was just looking for a suitable place to jump out, preferably a soft landing, when the bicycle stopped and a young lady leaned over the basket, looking right at him. She looked more surprised than he was, but then she smiled and told her friend, a man on another bicycle, and the two of them got their phone cameras out. Clancy wasn't interested in any more selfies, and jumped out onto the road. He turned back to see the two cyclists waving and smiling at him. He gave them a little smile and they rode away.

Heading along the road at a slow hop, Clancy had no idea where he was, or how to get home. It wasn't as simple as just turning back, as the cyclists had taken many turns and side roads. Up ahead he could see what he knew must be the Thomson Bay settlement (a small town square). His parents and other older quokkas had told him about it, and how he should do his best to avoid it. From what Cobba had told him, the quokkas of the Thomson Bay Clan sounded like rascals. But none-the-less, he had to go to the settlement to get directions home. He hoped he could find some friendly quokkas, but he knew he would have to be on his guard.

He hopped along the road towards the settlement, gazing up at the enormous branches of the fig trees that hung overhead. He'd never seen such enormous branches.

The delicious smell of baking bread wafted over from the settlement and Clancy's tummy rumbled. Even though he knew he mustn't eat it, freshly baked bread sure smelled good. But he would have to settle for a nice juicy shrub and was just looking around at the local plant life when a burst of bells rang behind him. Clancy turned to see a four people on segways zooming around a corner, straight for him. He jumped off the road and watched in wonder as they swept past so smoothly, it looked as if they were gliding.

"That was close," he said to himself, "I've got to keep my wits about me."

He was getting closer to the town when he spotted a delicious, juicy looking purple berry on the ground in front of him. *What a stroke of luck*, he thought. He hopped over, took it in his paws and chomped down. Something white flashed in front of him with a *whoosh* and the berry disappeared. He saw the culprit perched on a wooden rail nearby: a seagull.

"Thief," he yelled at the bird, who lifted its head and swallowed the berry whole. "Why don't you find your own food?" he asked. The seagull looked down its beak at him, then turned and flew away.

Chapter 4

Clancy came to the settlement, where the delicious smell of baking bread and pastries was stronger than ever. There was a very pleasant sound coming from the settlement, something Clancy had never heard before. It was music, and he could see it was coming from a lady sitting on a chair in the middle of the square, singing as she played along with a guitar. Clancy was entranced by the beautiful music. Some members of his clan were fond of drumming branches on rocks, which was enjoyed by all, but he'd never heard music before, and found it quite hypnotic. He looked around in wonder. There were more people than he'd ever seen in his life, perhaps forty or even fifty. Most were sitting on benches and at tables, beneath trees that were spaced out to provide the square with plenty of shade. Other people were bustling in and out of shops and taking selfies with quokkas. Nearby, huddled under a table that was occupied by four people, three quokkas seemed to be having a serious chat. Clancy hopped over and, careful to keep his distance from the people, he poked his head under the table.

"Excuse me," he tukked. The other quokkas didn't seem to notice and continued speaking among themselves. He thought perhaps they hadn't heard him, as there was plenty of noisy chatter from the people at the table. He tried again. "Hello."

They turned to him.

"Would you mind helping me? I need to find—"

They looked away from him and continued chatting in a manner that was so fast, Clancy could barely understand a word of it.

"Sorry to interrupt you," Clancy said, "but I need to find my way back to my clan. It's the Basin Clan, do you know it?"

The three quokkas looked at him like he was a nuisance, and hopped away without saying a word. *Boy*, he thought, *the quokkas of Thomson Bay are not a very friendly mob*.

Clancy walked along the edge of the square, keeping his distance from the people, who seemed to be coming from all directions. Beneath the shade of a tree, Clancy spotted a young quokka being bullied by a large, heavy set quokka. Bullying was something that his clan would not tolerate and, seeing the big quokka pushing the youngster to the ground repeatedly, Clancy felt obliged to help.

"I'm sorry, Choppa," the little quokka said to the larger one. "I'll try harder."

Clancy hopped over and stepped between the two quokkas.

"Hey Choppa. That is your name, right?" Clancy said. The big quokka snarled at him. "I think the little guy has had enough," Clancy said. Choppa was a several paws taller than Clancy and looked meaner than any quokka he'd ever seen, with sharp teeth, piercing eyes, and patches of fur missing from his head and shoulders. A ripple of fear ran through Clancy's body and he almost wished he had minded his own business. But those thoughts vanished when he looked back at the young quokka cowering on the ground. "Now's your chance," Clancy whispered "get out of here."

Then he turned back to Choppa, who was breathing his rotten, smelly breath down on Clancy.

"I'm Clancy, from the Basin Clan. Nice to meet you."

A low growl came from Choppa's throat, and his big bulging eyes looked as though they might pop out with rage.

"I can see you're busy. If you could tell me how to get back to the Basin, I'll be on my way."

Choppa's eyes widened with rage and he puffed out his chest and lifted his clenched front paws. Before he could strike, something appeared between them–a piece of hot bread, dangling from the hand of a human. It was the most delicious thing Clancy had ever smelled. Choppa snatched it away and gobbled it down.

Clancy put a paw on the little quokka's shoulder and was guiding him away when another piece of bread appeared before his eyes. He looked up to see another person trying to entice him to take a selfie. He turned away, only to have more bread shoved in front of him. It seemed everywhere he turned, someone was trying to feed him something in order to get a photo. Feeling overwhelmed, he found a gap between some peoples' legs and bolted.

Clancy took cover beneath a wooden bench and looked out at the dozens of people wandering in all directions, and four young quokkas who were vying for their attention. Choppa stood close behind them. The little ones took the food that was offered to them, posed for a selfies with the people who had given it to them, then handed the food to Choppa, who devoured every skerrick.

"So that's his racket," Clancy said. "He makes them get his food." He kept watching, and noticed that when the young quokkas looked tired and miserable, Choppa would give them a shove in the back, and they would force a smile. This scene made Clancy angry, and he wondered if there was anything he could do about it. Before he could think of anything, a young lady's face appeared right in front of him.

"Here's the cute one!" she said, sticking a phone in front of Clancy's face. She snapped a photo, setting off a bright flash. Clancy was blinded for a moment, and shook his head, blinking his eyes until his vision began to return. *These people don't quit!* Clancy thought. A few more people appeared in front of him.

"I think the little fella's had enough," someone said, "come on, let's leave him be."

They turned and walked away and Clancy felt greatly relieved. But only for a moment. When the people cleared, he saw Choppa standing in front of him, grinning an evil grin.

"Oh, pelican pee," Clancy said, as Choppa shuffled up before him.

"From the Basin Clan, hey?" said Choppa, a menacing smile on his face.

"Yes, do you know it?"

"Of course! I'm from the Basin."

"You are?"

"Indeed. I enjoyed life at the Basin, but it was a bit too quiet for my liking. Still, I do miss Kenneth and the Clan."

"Kenneth is my dad!"

"Is that right?" Choppa said, a hint of fear coming over him, which he quickly disguised. "Well, we will have to get you back to your clan, won't we?"

"Oh, that would be great; my mum will probably be having a fit about now."

"I'd be happy to help. But first, perhaps you could do me a favour?"

"Sure."

"The people seem to like you very much. You're a handsome young fellow," he said with a wry smile.

"I don't know about that," Clancy said, blushing.

"Nonsense, you're too modest," Choppa said, leaning closer. The smell of his warm, filthy breath made Clancy feel queasy, and he turned his head to one side, trying to avoid the brunt of it. "What can I do for you?" Clancy asked.

"It's getting close to lunch time and I've barely had a bite. Would you...?"

"You want me to get food for you? Like those young quokkas?"

"I think you'd be very successful."

"Don't you know people-food isn't good for?"

"Hmm, I know that's what Kenneth and your clan think, but I can tell you there is nothing more delicious than people-food. It hasn't done me any harm."

"Well," Clancy said. He was about to mention that Choppa didn't look very healthy, with patches of fur missing and gaps in his very sharp, black and brown teeth. But he doubted Choppa would listen to him, and thought the quickest way for him to get home would be through polite co-operation. "I suppose I could give it a go," Clancy said.

Moments later, Clancy and Choppa were standing in the middle of a busy crowd. It wasn't long before Clancy caught the eye of some passersby, and the next thing he knew he was being handed a bite-sized piece of pastry. As much as he loved the smell of it, seeing what it had done to Choppa had put Clancy off people-food for good. He put it behind his back and Choppa swiped it out of his hand and gobbled it up, as the girl with the phone crouched down and took a selfie.

"Oh no!" she said to her friend, inspecting her photo. "the ugly one photo-bombed me!"

On the photo on her screen, Clancy could see Choppa leaning behind her, his big, yellow eyes bulging and his mouth wide open as he shoved the food down.

The girl's friends laughed. "He looks more like a rat than a quokka!"

"Try to get a selfie with the cute one," the friend said.

Clancy felt a bit sorry for Choppa, but the big quokka wasn't concerned about what people thought. He shoved Clancy in the back. "Get some more!"

Clancy turned away from the girls, and just as he expected, they offered him some more food to make him look up to the camera. He took the food, a tortilla chip, and dished it back to Choppa, looking up to the camera. The girls snapped away.

"Aw, gorgeous!"

"How adorable!" they said, and walked away, only to be replaced by the next group, who had their phones out and ready. This went on for some time and Clancy soon became an expert at playing coy, getting some food and smiling for the camera as he dished it off to Choppa, who seemed to have an endless appetite.

Finally, Choppa tapped Clancy on the shoulder. "Okay, kid, I'm stuffed."

"Thank goodness for that!" Clancy said. "Now will you show me the way back to the Basin?"

"All in good time, kid. First, I need to take a nap. All this eating has made me tired."

"How long are you going to sleep for?"

"Not long. Just an afternoon nap," Choppa said.

Clancy watched as people stepped aside, making room for Choppa, who headed to a shady spot beneath a tree, curled up and went to sleep.

"Great," Clancy said.

"You there," came a voice behind him. He turned to see an old grizzly looking quokka, similar in appearance to Choppa, just as mean and unhealthy looking. "I'm Whipper; been watching you. You've got a certain, irresistible charm. People can't help but give you food. So you'll work for me, now that Choppa's had his fill."

"Ah, no thanks," Clancy said.

Whipper grabbed Clancy by the fur on the back of his neck. Clancy wriggled free and as the quokka lunged at him, he ducked out of the way and bolted. Looking over his shoulder, he could see the huge quokka hopping after him. Whipper followed him as he weaved around trees, between passing cyclists, and through a line of people outside an ice-cream shop. Clancy ran into the middle of the square, where he hoped to lose the big quokka in the crowd. He turned and crouched, looking through the passing people. The big quokka stood at the edge of the square, big bulging eyes darting left and right, then finally finding Clancy. The beast of a quokka set off sprinting through the crowd, making a line for Clancy, who sprang up and bolted. He headed to the entrance of the General Store. On the plastic saloon doors was a picture of a quokka with a line through it, which clearly indicated that quokkas were not welcome. *Probably the safest place to go,* Clancy thought, and burst through the flapping doors with a bang, Whipper hot on his tail. The two quokkas dashed down the aisle, causing quite a commotion as people scattered out of their way. Clancy raced around a corner where he could see dozens of quokkas sitting on shelves staring straight at him. He quickly realised they were stuffed toys, though they looked real enough. Knowing the big quokka would be bounding around the corner any second, Clancy leapt up onto the lowest shelf, amongst the soft toys. He turned and sat up on his bottom, trying his best to look like one of his stuffed companions.

Whipper slid around the corner then stopped. He looked over the toy quokkas, inspecting them closely. Clancy didn't so much as breathe, keeping perfectly still, eyes straight ahead. The big quokka sniffed at the toys, punching them with his paws as he passed over them, getting closer to Clancy. Though he wanted to look around for the best escape route, Clancy didn't dare move so much as an eyeball. But soon Whipper was just a couple of stuffed toys away and Clancy knew he was going to have to make a run for it.

"Oi," came the voice of a woman wielding a broom. "No quokkas allowed," she said. The big quokka panicked and fled through the exit doors. Clancy kept still as the woman looked over the toy quokkas, straightening them after Clancy and Whipper had messed them up. She looked Clancy in the eyes.

"You can't fool me," she said. Clancy's heart sank as she leaned closer. She had a kind face and he wasn't afraid for long. "You're safe now, he's gone. Out you get."

Clancy hopped down from the shelf and turned back to her.

"Hop along, little fella," she said with a smile.

And so he did.

Chapter 5

Clancy stalked around the square, keeping an eye out for Whipper as he went in search of Choppa. Sleeping or not, Clancy needed to get directions from Choppa so he could find his way home. *Now!* In the shade beneath a shop awning he came across a gathering of kindly looking quokkas who were busy chatting.

"Er, excuse me," he said.

"Yes, dear?" one of them said. She reminded him of his mother and Clancy felt a sudden pang of homesickness.

"Do you happen to know the way to the Basin?"

"No, dear," she said. "You ought to ask Choppa. He knows his way around the island."

"Yes, he does," agreed another quokka, "but whether or not he tells you is another matter."

"True, very true," said the first quokka. "He's not the friendliest quokka, is he?"

Clancy spotted Whipper walking in his direction, though the big quokka hadn't seen him yet.

"Thanks," said Clancy.

"You're welcome, dear. Good luck!"

Clancy scuttled along in the shade and soon came to the place where Choppa had been sleeping. But he was nowhere to be seen.

He looked around the square, which was even busier than before, and finally spotted the big quokka in the centre, shoving a couple of younger quokkas in front of a group of people. Clancy noticed that one of the young quokkas was the one Choppa had been bullying earlier. He looked miserable, and so did the other little quokka. Clancy made his way up to Choppa and tapped him on the shoulder.

"Not now!" said Choppa, before turning and recognising Clancy. "Oh, it's you. Come back to do some more work, hey?"

"No, it's time for me to go home."

"Go on, then, I'm busy here," Choppa said, snatching a piece of food from one of the younger quokkas.

"You said you would tell me the way home."

"And I will. But I'm hungry again, so if you can get me another good haul of food, I'll show you how to get home."

"We had a deal," Clancy said, as people began to gather around him with their cameras poised.

"Look, they're offering you food, kid. Grab it! Then I'll show you where to go."

Clancy didn't trust Choppa, but he felt he had no choice. Gritting his teeth, he turned to the gathering of people and was immediately confronted with a dangling biscuit. He took the biscuit, forced a smile for a selfie, and handed the food over to Choppa, who was salivating.

"So tell me, how do I get home?" Clancy asked him.

"You call that a haul? Get me some more."

"I'm not getting you any more food."

"Come on, kid," Choppa said.

"No. Tell me how to get home."

"Look, the people love you. Come on, just one more treat."

Clancy looked over the two younger quokkas, who were both smiling for selfies, but neither looked happy as people pushed and shoved to get closer to them, bumping them around.

"Alright," Clancy said. "One more treat, but you have to give these kids a break."

"Sure, sure. You get me a nice big treat and I'll leave these kids alone," Choppa said, "until I'm hungry again," he muttered under his breath.

Clancy turned to the crowd and gave them his warmest smile. A moment later he was surrounded by people vying for his attention. But as a young lady positioned herself to take a photograph, Clancy looked down to the ground, spoiling what the lady had hoped would be the perfect quokka selfie.

"Come on, little guy. Look up here at the camera? Please?"

But Clancy refused. The lady shoved a hand inside her handbag, dug around, and pulled out a cereal bar. She held it in front of Clancy's nose and he could smell the sweet honey and nuts. He looked up and tried to take the bar, but she lifted it higher, just out of reach. Clancy sprung off the ground with his hind legs and snatched the bar out of her hands. The lady gasped, dropping her phone.

That's what you get for feeding quokkas! Clancy thought, as he handed the bar over to the drooling Choppa. "Now, how do I get home?" Clancy demanded.

Choppa gorged himself on the sweet bar, crumbs spilling down the side of his mouth. The two smaller quokkas fed on whatever crumbs spilled onto the ground.

"Take the road away from the square. Follow it all the way until it divides into two, then go straight ahead into the bush."

"You mean, leave the road?"

"That's what I said, isn't it? Keep going through the bush for about a thousand hops, and you'll end up at the Basin. And if you don't, you're always welcome back here," Choppa said, chomping away.

Clancy leaned down to the young quokkas. "You really shouldn't eat human food."

"Get outta here!" Choppa said.

Clancy took a last look at the little quokkas, who were still cute and healthy, despite their diet of human food. He looked back at Choppa, who along with Whipper, was easily the most unhealthy looking quokka he had ever seen. He hoped the little ones wouldn't end up like Choppa, but thought they probably would. He turned towards the road, keen to get home, and hopped his way through the moving maze of human legs, which seemed to be everywhere.

Soon he made it out of the bustling square to the winding path, which was shaded by overhanging trees. Relieved to finally be on his way, he set off at a brisk hop, energized by the thought of being back with his clan. He passed the several pedestrians, both humans and quokkas, and a few cyclists, before coming to a fork in the road, where he stopped.

"Go straight ahead, into the bush," Clancy said, repeating Choppa's words. But the bush was dense and he didn't see any sign of other quokkas inside. Still, he didn't seem to have any other choice, so he wandered off the road, ducking beneath low-hanging branches and going around thickets and bushes.

Chapter 6

S ome of the bushes were sharp and dug at his sides, scratching him, but Clancy forged ahead for what seemed like a very long time. The terrible sound of a bird in distress stopped him in his tracks. Clancy's ears pricked up, as did the hair on his back. After a quick assessment, he shot off in the direction of the squawking.

He made it into a clearing where he saw, a few feet above the ground, the red-capped robin stuck in a thick spider's web that stretched between two trees. It was the biggest web Clancy had ever seen and he guessed it was about ten quokkas wide. The robin was desperately wriggling and squirming and squawking, and for good reason. A large, hairy wolf spider was making its way along the web towards him. It would probably already be sinking its fangs into the beautiful bird, if it weren't for the golden whistler that was hovering just above. The whistler continuously swooped down and tried to peck it, distracting the spider, which in turn tried to bite the bird.

Clancy had to act fast. These two birds had been very helpful to him when he was stuck in the basket on the bike, and he was more than happy to return the favour. But he didn't know quite what to do. The robin squawked like it was screaming for help. Clancy jumped up the trunk of one of the trees so he was right beside the web. With an outstretched paw, he tried to grab the robin, but he couldn't quite reach.

The spider realised that if it leaned on its back legs, fangs in the air, it could keep the whistler at bay while running towards the robin. As it got closer and closer to its prey, Clancy pointed his backside towards the bird, trying to reach it with his outstretched tail. But it was still no use. He turned back and saw the spider sprinting towards the bird, its fangs primed to strike. As it closed in, Clancy's instincts took over and he leapt from the tree trunk, straight at the spider.

The wolf spider sensed him coming and redirected its fangs at Clancy, who shot towards it like a flying furball. Clancy crashed through the web, taking the spider with him as he hit the ground rolling. He had a hold of the spider's legs, keeping his paws well clear of its fangs, which were snapping furiously. Clancy slammed into a log and the spider flew from his paws, landing on the dirt a few feet ahead. It shook itself to clear its head, then scowled viciously at the young quokka.

Clancy looked back at the robin, who had fallen on the leafy ground and was still tangled in web. The whistler tugged at the web with its beak, struggling to free its red-capped friend.

Clancy tried to leap up to help, but couldn't move. One of his back legs had skidded under the log and was stuck.

The spider saw all this and scuttled along the ground past Clancy, heading for the robin.

Clancy shook and wriggled and kicked, trying to get the log off his leg, as the spider got closer and closer to the bird. Leaning into the log, Clancy dug his front paws beneath it then pushed with all his might. He lifted the log off the ground and pulled his leg out. He turned to see the spider sprinting towards the birds, its fangs ready to attack. With a mighty leap, Clancy sprang off the ground, right over the top of the spider, landing beside the red capped robin. Clancy and the golden whistler worked together, pulling the web off the red-capped robin. There were only a few strands left when Clancy turned to see the wolf spider leaping off the ground towards the robin. Clancy leaned back on his tail and used both feet to kick the spider, sending him flying high over the bushes and out of sight.

The birds chirped in applause, the robin now free and hovering with the golden whistler above Clancy. They seemed to be smiling and Clancy smiled back. They swooped down, nuzzling against his back and chest as they circled him.

"Do you know where the Basin is?" Clancy asked.

They both pointed their wings in the same direction. Clancy looked through the bush and could see the ocean. He wasn't far now.

"Thanks," he said to them. They winked at him, then flew away.

Something was troubling Clancy. He remembered Van Cleef's words, "when a youngster needs help, you must do your best to help them. Don't hope that someone else will. We quokkas need to take care of each other."

He turned around and headed in the opposite direction, back towards the Thomson Bay settlement.

Chapter 7

Before long, Clancy was back at the settlement, dodging segways, bicycles and pedestrians, and avoiding quokka selfies. He soon found the young quokkas who, under the watchful eye of Choppa, did their best to charm the visitors, taking food in return for selfies. Choppa was gorging himself, the youngsters feeding on the crumbs he spilled. Clancy stepped in amongst them.

"Ah, you're back!," Choppa said. "Couldn't stay away, huh? You've come at the right time."

"I didn't come back to work for you, I came to help these kids. You quokkas need to stop eating people-food," Clancy said.

"Hey! Take it some place else, mate!" said Choppa.

"Where are your parents?" Clancy asked.

The little quokkas shrugged. "We come from the Lake Clan, but we don't know how to get back home."

"I bet we can find it. Come on, let's go!"

Before he could lead them away, Clancy hit the pavement hard.

"You ought to mind your own business," Choppa said, standing over him, his tail poised to strike again. Clancy saw a cookie lying on the ground beside him. He grabbed it and tossed it behind Choppa. The big quokka pounced on it, and Clancy grabbed the two young quokkas by the paws and led them away, hopping through the crowd.

"Get back here!" Choppa called, chomping on the cookie. "You bring those young quokk–" Choppa started choking on his food. He coughed and spluttered, and by the time he was okay, Clancy and the young quokkas were nowhere to be seen.

CLANCY LED THE YOUNGSTERS around a corner, where they introduced themselves. They were Cody and Courtney.

"So you're from the Lake Clan, hey?"

"Yeah. But we don't know how to get back there," Cody said.

"There's a map of the island over there, but we don't know how to read it," Courtney said.

They walked over to the map, where Clancy could see the whole island laid out, with a caption.

"You are here," Clancy read. He looked over the map, then at his surroundings, and soon he understood exactly where they were on the map. He scanned it carefully and located the lakes, and a road that led the way.

"I think we can get you guys home," Clancy said.

"There are more quokkas working for Choppa's brothers," said Cody.

"How many brothers does he have?" Clancy asked.

"Two: Whipper and Crusher," said Courtney. "Do you think you can rescue the others, too?"

"We can try," said Clancy. Whipper was a lot faster and meaner than Choppa, and Clancy was a bit scared of him. He hadn't met Crusher, but just the name sent shivers down his spine. But he had to rescue the youngsters. "Okay," said Clancy, "let's go."

CLANCY, COURTNEY AND Cody crouched on top of a low wall that gave them a good view over the bustling square. It wasn't long before they spotted Whipper, who was whipping a young quokka with his tail and forcing him to take selfies for food.

"That little quokka being whipped is Spring," said Courtney, "known for being fast."

"That's good to know," said Clancy.

On the other side of the square they spotted Choppa talking to another big quokka, who looked even meaner than both Choppa and Whipper.

"That big one is Crusher," Cody said.

"I thought so. Is he fast?"

"Yeah, super fast. But only over short distances. He gets tired pretty quickly," Courtney said.

Crusher frowned and scratched his chin as he chatted with Choppa, keeping an eye on another young quokka who was busy working.

"What do you know about the other little quokka?" Clancy asked.

"That's Dimples, known for...being cute."

"Right. What in the world are those things?" Clancy asked

"They're peacocks, Courtney said. "You don't want to get them mad."

"Why not?" Clancy asked.

"Because they make the worst noise you've ever heard in your life. They are scary. Really scary."

"Really?"

"Really."

"Interesting," Clancy said. He looked around and noticed several seagulls that were skulking around the square. "Those seagulls will be here all day, I guess. Is that right?"

"Yep. As long as there are people around, they'll stick around."

"Good. I've got an idea. We're going to have to work as a team. First, we're going to need to get a quokka selfie."

CLANCY AND CODY SAT in the middle of the square and it wasn't long before a couple of people came, wanting selfies.

"I think they want something to eat," said one of the people.

"We mustn't feed them," said the other, "it's very bad for them."

Clancy was glad to hear this, but right now he needed some food—it was part of his rescue plan. He gave Cody a nudge and the two of them hopped along to another group of people, and before long they were given several muffin pieces each in return for some memorable quokka selfies.

"Okay, that should be enough. Let's get into position," Clancy said.

They walked over to the centre of the square and sat by a tree, paws full of muffin pieces. To one side, Choppa and Crusher were busy forcing Dimples to work for food. On the other side of the square, Spring was handing up food to Whipper. Careful to stay out of sight from the two bullies, Clancy and Cody looked up to Courtney, who was still perched on top of the low wall.

"Now we just have to wait," said Clancy. "Shouldn't be long." They looked around the square, which was busier than ever. Clancy noticed several seagulls sitting on the branches of nearby trees, hoping to scavenge some food scraps. "Perfect," Clancy said.

SITTING TIGHT ON TOP of the wall, Courtney was following Clancy's instructions and looking for cyclists. She noticed a group of three segways approaching the square from the north side.

"Three segways," she said to herself, "that'll do, I suppose. Now how about the south side?" She looked to the south of the square. No sign of any segways. Then a pair of cyclists appeared, also heading to the square. "Perfect," she said, and looked down at Clancy and Cody, giving them the thumbs up. But Clancy and Cody were busy and didn't notice her.

"I JUST HOPE THOSE SEAGULLS aren't afraid of three monster quokkas," Clancy said.

"Look!" said Cody, pointing up to Courtney, who was waving both paws frantically, trying to show them two thumbs up.

"Okay, here goes," said Clancy.

The two quokkas split up, Clancy heading towards Choppa and Crusher, Cody towards Whipper.

"Hey Dimples!" called Clancy, "You wanna go home? Come with me!"

Dimples looked at Clancy, then back at Crusher and Choppa.

"Clancy," said Choppa, "you're in pelican poop, now!"

Both Choppa and Crusher stormed towards Clancy, who hurled his muffin pieces at them. They stopped, not sure if they should grab the muffin pieces or grab Clancy. Crusher couldn't resist the food, and started scoffing it down. But he was soon surrounded by a swarm of seagulls that swooped and pecked at him, trying to make him drop the food.

Meanwhile on the other side of the square, Cody threw his muffin pieces at Whipper, who was also surrounded by a flock of swooping seagulls.

"Come on, Spring!" Cody called, and the little quokka joined him, hopping to the centre of the square, where they met Clancy and Dimples. Choppa was coming their way at full speed, a furious look on his snarling face.

"Let's go!" called Clancy, taking Dimples by the paw. He led the way as they jumped up onto the low wall, where Courtney had been moments earlier. Choppa bounded up after them, followed by Whipper and Crusher. Clancy noticed the group of three segways gliding through the square in one direction, and the two cyclists approaching from the opposite direction.

Still holding Dimple's paw, Clancy leapt from the wall onto a table, followed by Cody. They jumped down to the seat, then onto the pavement. Whipper, Crusher and Choppa were right behind them. The three young quokkas crossed the paths of the converging segways and cyclists, leaping onto the other side. The three bullies had to stop and wait for the segways and cyclists to pass, which gave Clancy and his friends a few valuable seconds to run further away.

They bolted around the corner of the general store, where two peacocks were grazing. The peacocks were taken by surprise. Clancy led the young quokkas between the two birds and down the road, where they met Courtney.

Choppa, Whipper and Crusher raced around the corner and got the fright of their lives. Screaming at them with their feathers now fully fanned were the two peacocks.

"Hahaha!" laughed Clancy, looking at the three frightened bullies. "That's what I call a Choppa stopper!" The young quokkas laughed, happy to see the tables turned on the bullies, for once. "We better fly," Clancy said, and they set off.

The bullies backed away and gave the peacocks a wide berth. They saw Clancy and the young quokkas racing down the road, and set off after them. Clancy led them into the bush and the young quokkas weaved between the trees and around the thickets.

CLANCY, COURTNEY, CODY, Spring and Dimples emerged from the bush onto the sandy shores of a pink lake. They stopped to catch their breaths.

"We're home!" said Dimples.

But before anyone else could speak, Whipper, Choppa and Crusher leapt out from the scrub.

"I'll thrash that Clancy," said Crusher.

The young quokkas set off again, the bullies right behind them. Dimples stumbled and fell to the ground, and Clancy turned to help. By the time he had pulled Dimples up off the ground, the three bullies had surrounded them. They were puffing and panting furiously, with hateful looks in their eyes.

Clancy thought he could probably make a run for it, but he would have to leave Dimples behind, and he wasn't about to do that. He looked down at the little quokka, who was quivering in fear as the bullies closed in. Clancy braced himself, preparing to fight.

But then the bullies backed off. Clancy couldn't understand it. He looked over his shoulder he saw Cody, Courtney and Spring leading the entire Lake Clan towards them. The adult quokkas of the Lake Clan hopped forward at great speed, and Choppa, Whipper and Crusher fled into the bush.

Clancy was greeted with a very warm welcome by the Lake Clan. The parents of the young quokkas wept with joy, as they had given up hope of seeing their youngsters again. The scene brought a tear to Clancy's eye, and he thought of his own parents. It was time to go home.

The Lake Clan elders thanked Clancy and told him he would always be welcome there. He was very glad to have helped, and as he hopped away through the bush, he wondered when he would see them again. Perhaps he would return with Cobba some day.

Chapter 8

It was getting late when Clancy emerged from the bush and arrived at the town square. He had to make his way to the fork in the road, where he would head into the bush, and hopefully find his way home. But it was getting darker by the minute and he wondered if he would be able to find his way through the bush.

He made his way to the road and was hopping along when he was struck in the side *CRACK!* by a long quokka tail. It was Choppa. Whipper and Crusher were standing nearby. Crusher gave him a hefty kick, and Clancy rolled off the path in pain. But he knew the pain was going to get a whole lot worse if he didn't move fast, so Clancy ran for his life, the three bullies dashing after him. He took the nearest road, hopping as fast as he could, but the three quokkas were faster. He had no obstacles to slow them down this time, and they had almost caught him when he found himself at the beach.

They followed him onto the soft sand, which was hard to hop through, and soon he found himself at the water's edge. If these quokkas were anything like the quokkas of the Basin Clan, they would not want to go into the water. Clancy thought that might be the only way to escape. He leapt from the sand over a wave and landed waist-deep in the water. Clancy turned to see the three bullies standing at the water's edge. He was right–they weren't about to go in the water.

"Go in and get him, Whipper," Crusher said.

"You go in! I'm not getting wet!"

"Me neither," said Crusher.

"We don't have to get wet. He can't stay there forever, can you Clancy?" Choppa said. "But we can wait here all night. And when you do come out..."

"I'll give him a belting," said Crusher.

"And when you're finished with him, I'll have a go," said Whipper.

The water was a lot colder than it had been in the morning, and Clancy wondered how long he could take it. He began to shiver, his fur standing up on end.

"Come on, Clancy," said Choppa, "might as well get it over with."

Clancy remembered the stingray he had met at the Basin. He wondered if the ray was anywhere nearby, and began tapping his hands in the water, trying to send a distress signal.

"What are you doing?" Choppa said. "Trying to catch a fish?"

Choppa and his mates roared with laughter. Clancy didn't care; he tapped away furiously as the other quokkas rolled onto the sand, laughing.

"I think he's asking the fish for help," said Whipper, as they laughed hysterically.

Clancy was getting tired from tapping and finally he gave up. He folded his arms, shivering.

"Enough is enough, Clancy. Come on out," Choppa said. Then Choppa noticed movement in the water behind Clancy.

"What in the world is that? You better get out of the water, Clancy. Really!"

Clancy turned to see the big stingray sliding in behind him, sweeping him off his feet. He sat on its back as it sped towards the shore, making a mighty wave that splashed the three bullies, soaking them through. The ray turned and shot out to the open sea.

Clancy leant down and tapped the ray on the back. "Just in time!" he said. "Can you take me home?" he asked.

The ray nodded its head and shot off along the surface of the water, the last rays of sunlight lighting the way back to the basin.

Chapter 9

Clancy was home in no time at all. The ray brought him right up to the beach, and Clancy climbed off its back.

"Thanks very much. You really saved my skin," Clancy said. "What's your name?"

The ray shook its head as if to say it didn't have a name.

"I guess Ray would be a good name, don't you think? Seeing as you're a stingray." The stingray seemed to like that name. "But you cut through the water like razor, so I'll call you Razor. How about Razor Ray?" Clancy asked.

The ray nodded enthusiastically, and Clancy could tell he was pretty happy with the name. "Okay, Razor Ray, I better get back to my family, they'll be worried about me. Hey, I'll see you tomorrow, okay?"

Razor nodded, and Clancy waved and said goodbye.

His parents were indeed worried about him, and were very glad to see him in one piece.

That night, Clancy sat around the watering hole with the entire clan, Cobba sitting beside him. They listened in amazement as he entertained them with stories of his adventures: helping the young quokkas; the Thomson Bay bullies; rescuing the red-capped robin; meeting the Lake Clan quokkas. He didn't mention Razor Ray, as he thought that might upset his parents, who did not want him going in to the sea. By the end of the story, they were all exhausted, none more so than Clancy. He went to bed early that night, dreaming of what other adventures awaited him on their wonderful home, Rottnest Island.

The End

From the Author

Thank you for reading Clancy the Quokka of Rottnest Island. I hope you enjoyed it.

If you did, please review it here[1]. Reviews are very important and helpful, and I would really appreciate reading one from you!

---

1. https://www.amazon.com/review/create-review/listing

Can you imagine meeting Clancy?
Imagine if you met him, and he
actually spoke to you! Better yet,
imagine if you were the only person he
ever spoke to, and it was your special
secret. Well, that's exactly what
happens to an eight-year-old girl
named Kylie. Not only does she speak
to Clancy, she goes on incredible
adventures with him. You can read all
about those adventures in the Rotto!
series.

When eight-year-old Kylie meets Clancy the quokka, her whole life changes! She discovers a secret quokka world, then joins Clancy on an incredible adventure, learning to have courage and believe in herself along the way. Get your copy today, and discover why boys and girls all over the world are falling in love with Rotto!

amazon.com[1]

amazon.com.au[2] amazon.com.ca[3]

amazon.co.uk[4] amazon.de[5]

amazon.in[6]

---

1. https://www.amazon.com/dp/B07CJD8DJQ

2. https://www.amazon.com.au/dp/B07CJD8DJQ

3. https://www.amazon.ca/dp/B07CJD8DJQ

4. https://www.amazon.co.uk/dp/B07CJD8DJQ

5. https://www.amazon.de/dp/B07XC3NC71

6. https://www.amazon.in/dp/B07CJD8DJQ

Kylie and Clancy must find an important old treasure, or the quokka clan will face certain disaster! Join Kylie, Clancy the Quokka and Razor Ray on a swashbuckling adventure the whole family will love!

amazon.com[1] amazon.com.au[2] amazon.com.ca[3]

amazon.co.uk[4] amazon.de[5] amazon.in[6]

Visit Clancy the Quokka on his Facebook[7] and Instagram[8] pages.

---

1. https://www.amazon.com/dp/B08639RVDJ

2. https://www.amazon.com.au/dp/B08639RVDJ

3. https://www.amazon.ca/dp/B08639RVDJ

4. https://www.amazon.co.uk/dp/B08639RVDJ

5. https://www.amazon.de/dp/B08639RVDJ

6. https://www.amazon.in/dp/B08639RVDJ

7. https://www.facebook.com/clancythequokka/

8. https://www.instagram.com/
   clancythequokka/?hl=en